Furious Lit Vol. 1
Tell Me A Story

Published by

Published by Read Furiously. First Edition.

ISBN: 978–1–7337360–6–0

Anthology
Short Stories
Poetry
Comics
Storytelling

For more information on *Furious Lit* or Read Furiously, please visit readfuriously.com. For inquiries, please contact samantha@readfuriously.com.

Edited by Samantha Atzeni and Adam Wilson

Read (v): The act of interpreting and understanding the written word.

Furiously (adv): To engage in an activity with passion and excitement.

**Read Often. Read Well.
Read Furiously!**

Dear Furious Readers,

We began this project in January 2020 with the sole purpose of bringing you our first themed anthology featuring talented voices we've had the pleasure to work with previously and new creators we have been lucky enough to feature for the first time. Like so many of you, we had no idea what was in store for us as the year continued.

We are so proud of this collection of stories, but we would be remiss if we didn't mention that the direction shifted in the wake of COVID-19. Everyone involved in this project worked tirelessly balancing creative duties with added personal responsibilities, health scares, and a general sense of uncertainty that we all seemed to share and yet were unable to communicate. Our first themed anthology has now become our own time capsule from our creators and from the behind the scenes team at Read Furiously.

Now more than ever, we understand the healing power of storytelling.

To everyone that has been affected, and continues to be affected, you are in our thoughts constantly. We hope this volume provides a brief respite from this strange time we find ourselves in.

We wish to thank all of our wonderful contributors for sharing a piece of themselves in this very vulnerable time.

As always, read often, read well.

We dedicate this book to the incredibly talented John "Jonathan" Lewis Elliott who left us too soon, and we offer this volume in loving memory of those who have lost their lives to COVID-19.

May your memories and your stories live on.

Table of Contents

Yes.

Now tell me a story.

One that moves.
        That twirls
    That peeks
                        aroun
corners.

One that remains a consta
friend.
One that remains patient u
we can pick it up again.

Tell me a story.

Mine is the same, made of comfort and warmth.
Told in my voice but echoed by the voices that came before.

Tell you another one?
Okay, but listen...

ce upon a time, we came to life
came to life once upon a time.
ce upon a time, we came to life
came to life once upon a time
ce upon a time, we came to life
came to life once upon a time.
ce upon a time, we came to life
came to life once upon a time
ce upon a time...
Okay, your turn.
SELL SCHREIBMASCHINEN ZÜRI
ENSDORFERSTRASSE 101   TELEPHON (051) 33 66 99

...

While Darwin Sings in the Background Like a Greek Chorus

Shannon Frost Greenstein

I thought it would feel different, Freedom.

I thought it would feel…just more *obvious*, you know? Something you'd never need to question, one of those things standing firmly at the foundation of our understanding of the world: "Today, there is gravity, plants are photosynthesizing, and we are all Free."

But…that's not really what it's like. So maybe I never really understood what Freedom is, what it's supposed to look like when it's no longer theoretical. Maybe I didn't really get why we were fighting in the first place.

They say we're Free; the television turns on of its own accord at the turn of the hour to remind us all, Freedom interrupting our dreams and spoiling our meals and filling my central nervous system with adrenaline. The advertisements on the sides of buses and the digital billboards along the highways all extol in pictures how Free we are, images of happy young adults lounging in the sun, so saturated with liberty they don't even wonder where books went or why no one writes them anymore.

I don't wonder that, either, come to think of it, but that's because I already know. I watched it happen.

Not many people are left who have seen what I have, and isn't that just the best kind of irony, when your biggest flaw becomes the *literal* reason you are still alive, when so many others are not? That's what I try to focus on when the Survivor's Guilt hits, when I can't help but think, deep in my wise mind, about life before and everyone I used to know.

Instead, I focus on irony, and survival, and the gratitude I still have to still be breathing. If not for my mental illness, after all, my scarlet letter, the symbol I bore in the internment camps that identified me as Unique —without my bevy of diagnoses and the atypical brain they created, I would not have my life. I would not have purpose. I would not have Lady.

I would, instead, be very much alone.

I sigh, as the television switches back to silence, as I am granted another 55 blissful minutes of sleep before I will hear yet again how we are the greatest democracy in the world; although they razed the world and redefined democracy, so it doesn't really feel like as much of an accomplishment as it would have before.

I hear a scuffle in the hallway, a noise that would be ominous if I didn't already know it was Lady; but these days, everything seems to be ominous, a far cry from how I had pictured Freedom from the other side of the Revolution, when I still thought it was only about inalienable rights, when I thought real truth was self–evident.

"Lady!" I call in what my former self's husband had called the "kitty–voice." "Lady, come to me!"

Lady is black as pitch, and furry, extremely furry, with tufts of fur growing from the tip of her tail at all angles like a sparkler, and above her eyes like cartoon eyebrows, and between her toes, so that she often slides off of whatever landing pad she's planned to jump upon and ends up in a pile on the floor. Lady rarely sticks a landing, and isn't that a great synopsis for life with mental illness, too?

"Come here, kitty," I invite, and she runs over to jump up next to me, kneading the blankets into a rough nest, eyes shut and sides vibrating. I feel a warm glow spread through me, until I am practically purring myself; I drift off, only waking when Lady springs off of my chest, claws extended, as the television blares to life and reminds us all of how miserable we were before the war.

It's odd, to think about it. I hear 24 times every day how miserable I used to be, and how lucky I am now, now that books are gone, never to return. And I can remember, too, the misery, flashes of anguish or grief or rage, days of tears, an overwhelming sense of futility. So I am not being gaslit; these memories are mine.

But you were sick, my wise mind occasionally tries to remind me. *You were sick and there was no healthcare at the end, so of course you were miserable.*

I answer it aloud, in those moments, banishing the thought, rife with treachery and the uncertainty that everything has been for the greater good, back into the depths of my unconscious, where it belongs.

"Everyone was miserable," I say, echoing the material on the only television channel, the songs the children sing in school, the daily pledges to a brand–new flag. "Nothing is more important than being Free," I insist, and when my wise mind tries to interrupt with questions about the nature of Freedom, I shut it right back down again.

Of course, my wise mind doesn't interrupt so much these days anymore. It's probably all the pills, but you know what? I prefer it. I prefer it to being manic or depressed, I prefer it to feeling out of control or dysregulated. I prefer it to how I used to feel –though, at this, I have to work extra hard to quiet my wise mind, which tries occasionally, even now, to fill my head with lies.

It tells me how I've been used, how I've been abused; medication–deprived and government–tested and finally selected as Unique, all in the name of Eugenics. *A lab rat*, says my wise mind, but I know enough not to pay attention to treasonous falsehoods. At the end of the day, there's not even much at all of my former life that I am capable of remembering anyway. It's probably the pills I get now, like I said.

###

I glance at the clock and see it is essentially time to wake up, anyway. I sit up, rub my eyes, search out Lady. She is hungry, I can tell, and impatient.

Lady Kitty. My everything.

When they rounded us up; when they pulled me aside in the squalor of the internment camp where they kept the revolutionaries after the war, even as they were telling us how Free we were; when I was saved from certain death because of my imbalanced brain chemicals, my mutations, the genetic blemishes that made me worth saving while so many neurotypicals were not worth anything at all; when I became nothing more than an evolutionary blueprint of what *not* to do; when they realized I could translate several languages with the eidetic memory that is the reward of my anxiety disorder, they rewarded me for my subservience and brain with a cat. With Lady.

She is valuable, all cats are valuable these days, and again with the irony: Like the mentally ill, like *I*, can possibly protect anything of value, when I can't even take care of myself. Lady is mine, and I am hers; she is my familiar. She is all I have, now that the birth rate is so heavily controlled; not like they'd let me add to the new pristine gene pool, of course, with the Eugenics Program holding sway over us all.

I am happy with this arrangement, though, I think. Provided I keep translating without asking any questions, I am allowed to live; I am allowed to be Free. Whatever Freedom really is, that is.

But I always thought Freedom would feel different, to be honest, and I never thought I'd get a cat; and I had literally no idea that Ray Bradbury was spot–on correct. But books *do* burn at 451 degrees Fahrenheit, and that process smells differently than I expected it to, too.

I lose myself in a morning routine that requires little thought and revolves around the cat first and foremost. I feed her and brush her the way she likes, because her fur is so long it will clump into mats without regular grooming, then sit and procrastinate over my coffee with Lady sleeping in my lap until the television blares and reminds me that Utopia cares about me.

I jump in the shower, late as usual, dry my hair, and hurriedly locate my keys. Then I take the handful of pills I am prescribed, the mirror in the bathroom equipped with a camera that always watches, to ensure I take them. They say it's for my Bipolar Disorder and anxiety, and I suppose it must be, because I no longer feel manic or depressed like I did before the war.

You don't feel anything now, my wise mind likes to argue. *They're keeping you docile. Bipolar Disorder doesn't require Thorazine.*

"Leave me alone," I know to say. "Utopia wants what's best for me."

There used to be a lot of information about Bipolar Disorder, remember? it occasionally tries again. *Remember the DSM–5?*

But THAT is just an unacceptable thought. Once a book —any book, now banned, now illegal, now widely known to be the true source of our misery before —is mentioned, I know to turn my brain off.

Things hurt less, somehow, that way.

I swallow the pills, check the clock, and groan, realizing I have about thirty seconds to stuff Lady in her carrier if I'm going to make the train to work.

"Lady!" I call out, searching for the likely hiding place of one cat in search of sunbeams or a respite from state–sponsored affirmations.

It's because so many pets died during the revolution that Lady is so special now; that all cats are so special. The veterinarians tried to explain why the dogs and guinea pigs and parrots and chameleons and chinchillas and pot–bellied pigs all died, tried to find out what in the nerve gas was poisoning them, but veterinarians were already a dying breed, and they no longer had any universities on which to rely. They were guessing, and we knew they were guessing, and they knew we knew they were guessing, so the government eventually just stopped trying to explain it and instead gathered up all the cats, the only remaining domestic companions, the species inexplicably unaffected by the chemical warfare, to distribute as currency or tokens of favor in the new hierarchy.

Lady and all the cats are such a blessing now, but only for now, and that might be the saddest part of this new normal, the insult added to all the injury of loss: That the only animals we have left to enjoy are not reproducing; they are sterile from the nerve gas, and soon, cats will be gone, like everything else.

Freedom isn't free, after all.

"Lady," I trill, my stress at the lateness of the hour seeping from the falsetto of my kitty–voice. "Lady, *seriously*, we have to go."

She walks haughtily out of the bathroom, and I reveal the treat I have hidden in my palm, something squishy and processed that smells vaguely of fish. She comes eagerly forward, at which point I grab her around her middle, manipulate her ungracefully into the carrier, toss in the treat, grab my keys, lock the door, and run like mad for the train, the train we are lucky to have, the television reminds me through the wood and locks as I depart, now that we are Free.

###

Lady saved me. Through the isolation, and then all the tests, the job training, the doctors, the Orientation

–propaganda, whispers my wise mind occasionally, and I shush it automatically –she was there, one of the only animals left, a constant source of unconditional love, and because of that, as we languish here in Utopia – *Fascism*, my wise mind tries to argue, and I respond with the conditioned thought of *Freedom!* –I am one of the lucky ones. Me. Bipolar, Borderline, Obsessive Compulsive, self–harming, history–of–suicidal–thoughts *me*. But that's it, isn't it? That's why I still have my life. As the Eugenics Program runs rampant, the chance for geneticists to map my genome, fuckups and all, has made my measly life worth sparing. It has made me worth a cat.

And that, I feel certain, is as good as it will possibly get.

It's really only at night that I think about books anymore.

"Lady!"

She opens her eyes lazily, regards me, chooses to ignore me, and shuts them again.

In the background, a familiar white noise, I hear the radio station through the speakers that are built into every identical cubicle. It plays constantly, ceaselessly, not music but the soothing assertions of Utopian Broadcasting, reminding us of all the wars before THE war, all the discord, Holocausts and Inquisitions and Trails of Tears, and, always, the books that were behind it all.

"Lady, *get up*. Let's go eat. C'mon. Let's go."

My kitty–voice sounds irritated, strained. It has been a long day at the office, and my medication is wearing off, leaving behind a wake of tumultuous, formerly–numb emotions.

She opens her eyes again, yawns, and rises slowly, stretching individual muscle groups and ligaments and toes, at which point I lose all patience and force her into the carrier, pushing on her haunches as she goes limp like a protestor, passive resistance made incarnate.

We exit the imposing tower of my office building, its sides clad in steel plates, its abstract shape throwing an enormous, amorphous shadow over the city block below. There has been an architectural revolution, meant to glorify the revolution and commemorate Utopia's birth, but sometimes, I suspect it's also meant to make us forget.

Walking amidst the monoliths and towering concrete monuments –imposing in form, intimidating in function, messages to future residents and an erasure of the past, the banks and government buildings and restaurants each their own work of art –it's easy to disregard the banks and government buildings and restaurants that once stood in their places. The blood stains scrubbed and the rubble cleared, these near–absurdist modernist structures seem to encourage us not to remember.

Look at what we can achieve, they say. *Look to the future.*

The day–to–day machinations of the Utopian machine blend together during my commute, and I am lost in the fog of routine until I hear Lady's voice.

It sounds urgent; alarmed. If she were a service animal from Before, it would have been an alert, precognition of an upcoming seizure or diabetic coma. As it is, though, she is my life support; I am meticulously attuned to her, and right now, she is telling me something.

"What is it, kitty?" I ask, not expecting her to answer, but she *does* answer. She mews again, and again, and begins batting at the door to the carrier, toes poking through the grid.

"Do you want out?" I ask her, thinking, for some reason, that she will answer this too, because I am starting to feel the same alarm that has so agitated Lady. This is the most isolated section of my walk home from the train, and I'm starting to feel like we are being watched.

"We're going," I tell the cat sternly, as if I am debating a toddler, but stop abruptly as she begins to throw her weight against the sides of the carrier, body checking the plastic, until I lose my grip and drop the cat, carrier and all, onto the ground.

"Jesus, Lady!"

Still sensing the presence of someone or some*thing*, beginning to share Lady's panic, I nevertheless unlock the carrier and edge open the door. She tears out, makes it a few yards, then stops abruptly, turns around, makes eye contact, and trills again.

"Show me, kitty," I say, absurdly, feeling ridiculous,

and yet understanding, because Lady is my familiar; and because I see she is acting instinctually, from her limbic brain, guided in every way by evolutionary biology while Darwin sings in the background like a Greek chorus.

Having confirmed that I am following her, Lady leads me down the street and towards the river, a grittier section of the city. We delve through the growing dusk, encountering no one, leaving behind the lights of town. I am now positive something is close behind us. I look back over my shoulder often, finally losing sight of the cat as we weave between darkening structures and increasingly derelict–looking buildings.

"Lady…"

My voice quivers as I emerge from an empty alleyway, looking around frantically for my cat, practically feeling the breath of some unknown entity against the back of my neck. I do not see her, and my fear grows. Without Lady, I could no longer be a part of the world at all; and Utopia has taken steps to ensure there is no easy exit for those who serve the Eugenics program.

"Lady?" I whisper, on the edge of mortal terror, a combination of the absence of my missing half and the knowledge that something behind me lies in wait.

Suddenly, I hear her voice again and I freeze, squinting my eyes in an effort to hear better, searching out for any whisper of sound, and waiting. Sure enough, I hear her again, and relief surges through me, a wave of dopamine.

I direct my ears, falling back on my training like

a muscle memory; my many years of translating words and interpreting voice inflections and listening for languages and all that which lies between the sentences spoken, the pregnant pauses; all that which falls between the lines.

I am getting closer.

Finally, following her trills, I rush around the side of an abandoned brick structure and run through its decaying entrance, a wide maw of no particular shape. Inside, in a far corner, I see Lady in an ocean of moonlight; and against her side, curled into a sphere the size of a tennis ball, imperceptibly breathing, lies a newborn kitten.

My mouth is agape.

There can't be any more kittens. The scientists said so, before we made them all stop studying cats and start studying Eugenics. Everyone knows…the cats are all sterile.

But there is indeed a kitten, a brand–new one, and as I struggle to comprehend how such a thing could even be possible, I notice something even more mind–bending; so bewildering, in fact, that I am shocked it took me more than a split second to notice it.

The corner in which my cat lies…*cats*, my wise mind corrects me hesitantly, as neither one of us has yet figured out what we are seeing…is lined, layers deep, with books. Dozens of books. More books that I have seen since before we even started daydreaming about Freedom, books as walls and floor in all directions, books covered with old boxes and crates and detritus, but books, and it takes my breath away.

In that second, I have a flash of insight, a Eureka moment of understanding, that all our suffering, all our misery, all we lost and all we fought for and all we were trying to achieve, was, in fact, all in vain.

This isn't freedom.

Freedom would be to pick up one of these books, dusty and grimy as it is, and crack it open, right here on the ground in this abandoned building. Freedom would be to take one home, to take them all, in fact, to roll in books like a bath made of the twenty dollar bills from Before, to rub them on my skin so I might read by osmosis, to make up for all the time with them I have lost.

"Lady, what did you find?" I ask, with wonderment, with admiration, with veneration and fright. "Did you find a little kitty?"

Lady looks up at me, pleased, and rests her chin against the kitten's skull as my mind spins in concentric circles, all of them involving torture, mutilation, punishment, but all of them also involving hope, light, possibility; all of them involving books, and books, and books.

I finally give in, and reach to my right to pick out a book at random. I wipe away a layer of filth and reveal a partial title, *Gone with the W...*, the rest of the cover lost to time and rot. I bring the paperback to my nose and inhale, inhale the scent of mildew and droppings and stale smoke and time, and under it all, the pages; the pungent, musty smell of dusty paper and water stains and the dried blood flecked over the book like glitter. I am lost for a moment, a sense memory, a Method actor remembering the libraries and book depositories of Before, an entire world I hadn't remembered or have been trained to forget, springing to life from the aroma.

It is the scent of freedom.

"YOU FOUGHT FOR FREEDOM, AND UTOPIA IS YOUR REWARD!"

I jump and let out a strangled yelp as the broadcast blares from somewhere across the river, drifting in through the broken windows, and I am immediately yanked back to the present.

Get out, my wise mind advises, having been atypically quiet while I was lost in memory. *Get the cats and get out now.*

"But…" I literally argue aloud in a scratchy whisper. "But what about…?"

Leave the books, it urges. *It's too dangerous.*

But I am free, now, now that I've remembered freedom, and thinking of leaving these books behind is giving me physical pain.

Nonetheless, I gently usher Lady into the carrier and, holding my breath at its fragility, place the trembling kitten beside her. I stand, peer over my shoulder, see no one and nothing. Still, I have to garner every ounce of my willpower to start walking, to risk everything, now that Pandora's Box has been opened, now that its contents will taint Freedom with all the misery we thought we'd banished inside during the revolution, all that misery we thought we'd abolished by flame.

I am nearly outside when I pause, look back, make a decision, and spin around on my heel before I can change my mind.

Wait, implores my wise mind, but I am guided by pure Id now, my lizard brain clamoring for instant gratification; it takes only a few seconds to grab a book, unidentifiable in my rush, and stuff it next to Lady's substantial bulk within her case.

I dash out, the carrier banging against my leg, retracing my steps and choosing blind turns when I cannot remember the path I took. Finally, the web of alleyways evolves into semblances of cobblestone paths and then asphalt avenues; I slow my steps to blend in, though the streets are empty and night covers all.

After what feels like hours, I make it home.

I kneel and release the carrier, Lady immediately darting into the room. I lift out the kitten I have already christened Little Kitty onto the carpet, watching it wobble and sniff the air. I reach in, grab the book, and look at what I have successfully acquired, a seed of promise, an acorn, a symbol of what once was and a sigil of the fights for the future. In the light, I can see the title plainly:

On the Origin of Species by Means of Natural Selection, or the Preservation of Favoured Races in the Struggle for Life

By Charles Darwin, M.A.,

Fellow Of The Royal, Geological, Linnaean, Etc., Societies;

Author Of 'Journal Of Researches During H.M.S. Beagle's Voyage Round The World'

I open the cover, drawing a breath, reaching out to stroke the pile of cats, and allowing myself, finally, to remember…

When on board H.M.S. 'Beagle,' as naturalist, I was much struck with certain facts…

THE END

The Little Girl by the Sea

Story by Adam Wilson
Art by Ellie Pickett

Once upon a time, in a village by the sea, there lived a most peculiar little girl.

Peculiar because unlike most children her age, who loved to spend their days playing in the waters along the shore ...

This little girl feared the sea far too much to ever venture off the sand.

All her life she was gripped by this fe[...]. And unlike most childhood concerns, wh[...] seem to diminish with age, this one o[...] seemed to grow.

il one day . . .
JEEZ IT'S HOT OUT.
IT'S SUMMER. WHAT DO YOU EXPECT?
WELL I DON'T KNOW ABOUT U, BUT I COULD SURE USE A SWIM
NO BRENNEN, DON'T! PLEASE DON'T!
HELP!!!!
OH MY GOD!
FISH CHIPS

I... I WAS JUST...
PLAYING AROUND.

I DIDN'T KNOW SHE
COULDN'T SWIM

Now this is not a tragic story, one of death or loss.
So there is no need to mourn for the little girl.

This is simply a story of moving on.

You see, though she may never have been able to put it into words, it wasn't the sea that brought such fear into the little girl.
She was simply afraid of what might come next.
Because even when we can not understand them, deep down we know those moments in our lives when change becomes inevitable.
A part of us can always feel when we must let go and embrace our future. Though truly, there may be nothing more frightening than that.
And as the last of the search parties slowly began to disperse, the little girl turned away from the shore ...

A new and exciting world lay before her, and any fears that may have remained seemed trivial at best.
THE END

–Creation
–The Garden
–The Process of Understanding

Victoria Tracy

The Creation

—found lines in a geology assignment

You are establishing knowledge,
which you can apply
to new concepts in history.
The primary purpose
is for you to articulate
why it is important to you,
why you think it looks the way it does.
      Be descriptive.

You do not need to understand
how everything came to be,
but you will have to explain it.

Every detail, no matter how seemingly
insignificant, is important.
Why did you choose this
mountain, stream, waterfall, beach?
      Help me visualize.

Human processes are changing
the way you experience
your lifetime.
Therefore,
I believe creating is important.

The Garden

> "O, How unlike the place from whence they fell."
> —John Milton

Cloaked in a blissful haze,
running through the garden,
we felt the overgrown dandelions tickle
the soles of our feet, the delicate scent of jasmine
whirling around us while the gentle hum of cicadas
vibrated in our ears. We splashed along
the warm, babbling creek oblivious to the secrets
floating through the water. Mimicking the movement
of happy ants, we marched on, giggling
as sticky pomegranate juice
dribbled down our chins,

but the moment your fingers brushed
my hand

we felt the air thicken
as lust shifted into sin
and our Eden collapsed.

Crumbling into fire–bellied screams
and rushing chaos,
your hands no longer seemed soft and pure,
now they felt heated, angry
and I scrambled
to shield my nakedness
from your greedy stare.

Together, we felt shame.

Somewhere the Heavens chuckled.
The arrogant laugh reverberated against our bones
as He saw what fools we were
to think that everything could've remained the same
if Adam and Eve didn't fall.

The Process of Understanding

I devoured a book.

(I'm thinking of ending Things)
And it says that once a thought has been thought
You can't take it back.

It is there.
Floating,
drifting.
Just like Ben before he meets Elaine.
It is there.
Eating through your brain
like maggots ripping away at the underbelly of an
infected pig.
A conspiracy theory pressing against your skull,
begging, pleading, screaming to be released.
Et Tu Brute?

The words will eventually tumble
Tumble
Tumble
on to your tongue,
grinding against your teeth,
slamming like waves breaking against the rocky shore,
stinging your ulcers like the backlash of Sour Punch
Straw dust.

Once a thought has been thought,
it will consume you.

And we will be driving.

Speeding down the highway,
peacefully nodding along to a Greta Van Fleet song.
You are the one.
Babe,
you are *the one*.
And I will look over
as the thoughts finally begin to burst,
and the words ooze out like neon puss,

and you will keep speeding.
No brakes, no wipers, just faster and faster.
I am thinking–I am thinking–I am thinking–
You have thought–you have thought–you have–
I am–You are–I am–You are–
I am–
We are
ending Things.

The Magic of
Fairies

Margaret Montet

Behind my grandfather's bright blue eyes lived an Irish storyteller's mind. He would sit in his armchair in Butler, New Jersey, with his pipe stand to his right and tell his stories to whatever grandchildren might be around. Through cherry–scented pipe aroma I would hear "Margie me gal, did I ever tell you about the time…?" When I knew him, he was a retired letter carrier with lots of time to put together his tales which seemed extemporized and customized for his audience. One in particular sticks in my mind, told as he rode shotgun in our family's Ford Granada with the bumpy plastic seat covers. My father drove through the hilly terrain of Northern New Jersey, and I sat in the backseat with my mother and Grandma. Grandpa told this tale about my father and uncles fighting off a tribe of hungry cannibals on a tropical island. My father and uncles were trying to avoid landing in the giant black stockpot the cannibals had set up over an open flame. I remember laughing so hard my sides hurt while the other adults rolled their eyes. I know the plot sounds dumb. It had to be my grandfather's storytelling that made me laugh.

I very recently realized that Grandpa's cannibal story sounds a lot like Robinson Crusoe. My father was cast in the Crusoe role, and Uncle Bill W. and Uncle Bill L. shared the duties of My Man Friday. Crusoe and Friday battled cannibals in much the same way as my father and the Uncle Bills in Grandpa's story. I can see Grandpa as a little boy reading this book, and then as a young father, reading it to my mother and her siblings. He had the air of an adventurer about him even if his days of adventure were mostly behind him when I, the youngest grandchild, finally came on the scene.

Grandpa told his stories with that wry wit and a blue–eyed sparkle as a true Irishman would. He never told (in my presence, anyway) traditional Irish tales which are so important to Irish culture. During my recent visit to that legendary lush green island, I heard many: go to a pub—hear a story. Go on a bus tour—hear a folk tale. Besides Guinness, Aran sweaters (I bought two), and Claddagh rings, folklore is probably the country's most notable export.

When I think back on my Ireland experience, it organizes itself in my mind into a musical form. Musical forms are my way of making sense of structure—I know these well from my days as a Music Theory major. My Ireland memories, now processed and organized by my musical mind, have emerged in a sonata–allegro form. (This is the form in which most Classical and Romantic symphony and sonata first–movements are composed. It's a standard template.) Dublin is the exposition, the most important 'stuff' of the piece. Ancient Tara is the development, because the ancient history builds upon what I had already learned about Ireland generally and Dublin specifically. Belfast, another Irish city, is the recapitulation because as an urban center it recalls Dublin. It is, of course, different, just as a musical recapitulation will differ from the exposition it recalls. Galway is the most Irish region culturally because of its location far west from where historic invaders and influences came ashore in the east. During this symphony of a visit, I was charmed by the indigenous folk tales and songs, and Galway seems to be the capital of folk. This is where we heard the most about fairies. There's my coda to finish off the movement.

Dublin: Exposition

I was in Ireland with my writing program. Eighteen students and eight or so faculty called Trinity College, Dublin, "home" for two weeks while we learned to tell our own stories. I was assigned a fourth floor dorm room, so every day I climbed those hateful stairs more than once to my aerie in the sky. Forgot a notebook for a lecture? Up I'd go. Need a sweater? Up, up, up those stairs. At the end of a busy day, (they were all busy with lectures, workshops, and exploration), I would relax in my spot which was level with the Trinity College tree canopy. From the common room across the hall I had a bird's eye view of Trinity's Parliament Square including the Campanile (the bell tower where our group would collect before heading somewhere) and the Main Gate. With my window open I could hear the frequent rain hitting the leaves on the tree just outside, and the music wafting up from Grafton Street, just outside the college's wall: an electric guitar mimicking the great rock guitar solos of decades past, drunken vocalizations from outside of the pubs, and on a few occasions an electrified violin. All of this was in the air up there.

On our first morning in Dublin, fellow teller of true tales Amy W. and I began exploration by way of a travel brochure walking tour. We found our way to St. Andrew's Church and the larger–than–life–sized statue of Molly Malone with her seafood cart outside the edifice. Locals call the statue "the tart with the cart" owing to the low cut of her bodice and the centuries–old rumor that she was a prostitute in the evenings after parking her seafood cart. The statue is a meeting place in Dublin; in fact we would meet our Northern Ireland tour bus there the following weekend. Molly Malone is a fictional character, created in Irish music halls. (So, if she was a prostitute, it was because someone created her thus. We can't fault her for that.) She's a young woman who sells seafood from a wheel barrow in the streets of Dublin just as her parents did:

> In Dublin's fair city,
> Where the girls are so pretty,
> I first set my eyes on sweet Molly Malone.
> As she wheeled her wheel–barrow,
> Through streets broad and narrow,
> Crying 'Cockles and mussels, alive, alive, oh.'"

I checked YouTube for a recording of this song. There are many, by artists such as the Dubliners, the Ferrymen, and Bono, but Sinead O'Connor's version touched me most. (Did my mother sing this to me? It sounds so familiar.) She sings the song slowly, staring into the camera (at me) and yells "Cockles" and "Mussels!" as a fishmonger would, into the air above her accenting the second syllables of 'cockles' and 'mussels.' As I watched Sinead O'Connor's ethereal interpretation of "Molly Malone," I realized, from the way her performance sliced through my ribcage and directly into my heart, that my mother probably sang this to me when I was very little. I don't have a concrete memory of this but instead a vague, abstract recollection. Music is an art form which is gone as soon as it is performed except for the parts we store in an abstract memory somewhere in our complex brains. Music is storytelling, too.

Amy and I continued on our walking tour, continuing past St. Andrews Church and the Molly Malone statue, through more of the city, and finally arriving at St. Stephen's Green. This park in the center of Dublin, commissioned in 1880, was filled with birds, extra–large herring gulls, pigeons, magpies, robins, and wrens: in the air, on the pond water, and on the ground. Suddenly, from the green–leaved Sycamore branches above our heads, a plop of true Irish–green bird poo landed in my hair, on my brow, on my clean purple shirt, and on my camera. I did my best to clean up with leaves as neither of us savvy world travelers had so much as a tissue.

Tara: Development

Concentric circular hills surround the Mound of the Hostages in Tara. The "hostages" here are children from various Druid families who were taken hostage to be raised in the king's house. This is important and sacred territory for Druids (ancient pagans of Ireland), Celts, and Christians, too, as Saint Patrick convinced the king here to let him preach Christianity in Ireland by the fifth century. On the day that our group toured the Hills of Tara we also popped over to Loughcrew. The skies were graying over and there were some menacing dark clouds coming our way. We climbed some steep rocky steps which led us to a grassy hill. My guidebook advises that this is a 30–minute walk. I remember our tour guide, Keith, telling us that there was a bench halfway up if we had to rest, but our reward at the top of the hill, near the cairn or burial mound, was a "better bench." My breathing became squeaky as we climbed this steep hill and the wind increased and heavy rain drenched us. I had to stop at the first bench. I sat there on the bench in my deluxe raincoat in the pouring rain to wait for my squeaky, asthmatic breathing to stop. Brianna and Chris waited with me saying they needed a rest, too, but I didn't believe them. Bob, our director, was there, asking: "You'll be okay to finish the climb after a rest, right, Margaret?" I was indeed okay after a rest, and continued up the steep, grassy mountain (actually it's a hill) to the relief of Bob, Brianna, and Chris. I skipped these details in my travel journal, but I remember them clearly now.

The elasticity of time characteristic of fairy tales had inserted itself into my own experience. When I finally arrived at the top of the hill my companions were taking turns crouching through the opening of the burial mound with tour guide Keith. This is a megalithic (meaning made of large stones) cairn dating back probably to 3300BC. It is part of a passage–tomb where multiple chambers are connected. Sliabh na Cailli is the Irish name for this site, and that translates to "mountain of the hag." According to legend, a giant hag had a load of rocks in her apron for some purpose in her garden, got tired, and dumped them here. The "better bench" Keith had promised us was the Hag's Chair, a stone formation that looks like a seat with carvings and gouges in it where the hag rested. The hag's rocks are the green gritstone boulders we see now around the landscape, and inside the mound. We saw carvings of suns inside the tomb. Keith told us that these sun carvings are placed so that rays from the summer solstice sun would hit them. As if on cue, the sun broke through the clouds that moment we were in the burial mound. We were close enough to the solstice (early July) to see the sun's rays hitting the sun carvings. That was worth the torturous climb.

Belfast: Recapitulation

I will always think of Northern Ireland as wet. Amy, Kathy, Rena, Katie, Erin, Rachel, and I, writers of fiction, poetry, and nonfiction, met at the Molly Malone statue by St. Andrew's Church in the wee hours of the morning to board a bus for a day tour of Belfast and Northern Ireland. We were curious: were there still bullets flying and bombs detonating? Those troubles had tapered–off, right? The bus was luxurious. Because of the luggage compartments underneath, those bus seats ride high above the road and give the rider the sensation of rapidly cruising through the country air…until the bus hits a bump.

Our bus driver, Derrick, told us a fine story as we approached a curiosity called the Giant's Causeway near Belfast. A giant named Finn MacCool (or Fionn MacCumhaill in Irish) lived near here in County Antrim. He was a warrior–hero and tales of his adventures were later told from the point of view of his son Oisín. These were called the Fenian Cycle. In Derrick the bus driver's story, Finn was feuding with another giant, Benandonner, from Scotland. Finn crossed the water via a causeway he had built out of stone (basalt) columns so that he could settle things with his enemy. Something happened—Finn got scared or Benandonner wasn't in—and Finn ran back to County Antrim. Mr. and Mrs. MacCool received word that Benandonner was coming for Finn and they saw this huge creature himself lumbering across Finn's causeway. Not wanting to fight such a large opponent, Finn jumped under a blanket in a cradle and his wife then convinced Benandonner that this huge baby was her youngest of fifteen. Her other enormous children were out hunting with their gargantuan father, she said. It worked: Benandonner ran back to Scotland scattering Finn MacCool's neatly constructed causeway into piles of broken rocks. We were now headed to this very Giant's Causeway! Towering cliffs, rocks of all sizes, and tall clumps of hexagonal columns of basalt rose out of the breakers and foam. I walked away with breathtaking and unique landscapes in my Nikon.

Derrick drove us on our luxury bus to Belfast. Besides the memories of violent troubles in that city that I had seen on the evening news in the past, my only connection is a sepia family photograph which I found in my mother's portion of my grandparents' things with "Belfast" etched in gold in the corner under the photographer's name. I don't know who the people are, but they were from Belfast and are related to me somehow and here I am in that same city. There's an Irish word for the kind of day we had in Belfast: doineann, which means foul weather and the stress it generates. We could have paid some extra money (British pounds here) to go on a narrated Black Taxi tour of the city, but we decided to explore on our own. Up to this point in Ireland, rain showers had been brief so we were optimistic. Days like this are called breaclá or dappled days. Sunny skies alternate with rain. Most Irish days are like this. But no, the Belfast day was an extended soaker. We were wet and cold. As I clung to the wet paper bag holding the sandwich and pastry I bought to eat when I got back to my dorm room aerie in Dublin, I listened to the other bus passengers tell the story of their fine taxi tour. They saw Belfast's famous murals and the Titanic Quarter where the famous luxury liner was built. Shoot. I missed it.

This daytrip would have pleased my storytelling grandfather as his and my grandmother's ancestors came from Protestant Northern Ireland, County Antrim to be exact, where the giant MacCool family lived.

Galway: Coda

Kathy and I rode the fast train from Dublin to Galway when our residency was over. The train cuts across Ireland's middle like a leprechaun's belt with the train averaging about 89 mph for the 129–mile trip. We were interested in seeing Galway, a part of Ireland less touched by Anglo influences and where one hears Irish folktales and the Irish (Gaelic) language more than other regions. While we were there, the Galway International Arts Festival was going on, and we could often hear Irish music from the streets or pubs wafting up to our hotel room. There were fiddles, Irish bagpipes, drums called bodhrans, flutes, and voices, and often soaring high above the other instruments was the tinny sopranino sound of a penny whistle which to my ear transforms this worldly music into the music of fairies. Galway also boasts a fine, central location for daytrips: Connemara, the Aran Islands, and the Cliffs of Moher were the three that Kathy and I enjoyed.

Galway has a rich Irish folk tradition owing to its geographic position far away from the influences of England, and thanks to the work of playwright and Galway native Lady Isabella Augusta Gregory (1852–1932). She promoted the arts, co–founded Dublin's Abbey Theater, and, inspired by her friends in the Gaelic League, Douglas Hyde and W.B. Yeats, volunteered to collect and edit volumes of folktales. She could speak Irish (Gaelic) as well as English and therefore had a particular interest in her native Galway region where Irish was still spoken.

Lady Gregory collected the following tale from an old man in Galway in 1902:

A man named Robin sold a cow at a Galway market and then had a wee too much Guinness afterward. Rather than go straight home, he found a spot in a barn and made a bed in a pile of straw. He woke during the night to see some men hiding stolen silver in the straw. In the morning Robin told the distressed townspeople. The good citizens retrieved the stolen goods and waited for the criminals to return for it.

Robin's landlord heard of his heroic deed and was convinced that if Robin's special powers were real, Robin should help him: "I will lock you up in a room for three days. If you can't tell me by the end of that time who stole my wife's diamond ring, I'll put you to death."

On the first evening, the butler brought Robin his supper. "There's one of them," Robin said, meaning that the first of three days was over. The butler, however, thought Robin was fingering him for the crime.

The cook brought the second day's supper: "There's two of them," Robin said, and of course we know he meant the second day was over. The cook conferred with the butler. Both were shaken, because they were, in fact, the perpetrators of the crime along with the housekeeper.

Sure enough, when the housekeeper delivered Robin's supper on the third night, he said, "There's the third," and the three jewelry thieves begged Robin to help them avoid justice.

Robin considered the situation and devised a strategy: "Go and find that big tom turkey outside and force the ring down his throat." The next day when the landlord asked Robin to reveal the identity of the thief, Robin advised the landlord to have the turkey cut open. (They were going to eat it anyway.) Sure enough, the ring was there, Robin was free, and the turkey was framed for the crime.

From Robin's town of Galway, Kathy and I took a bus tour of the Connemara region, home to thousands of black-faced Connemara sheep, peat bogs, gothic Kylemore Abbey (home to Benedictine nuns who fled Belgium during World War I), and lots of talk of fairies. Our bus driver, Martin, had a strange but pleasing way of drawing out the last syllables of sentences as he prattled on nonstop about the sheep, the Burren, the bogs, and the fairieeeeees. Fairies have no past or future and therefore have no hopes, regrets, or memorieeeeees, but they do have the ability to speed up and slow down time. Mythical invaders condemned the fairies (called Sidhe in Irish) to live underground or in trees or bushes. They frolic in merry groups around hawthorn treeeeees. At one point, Martin pulled the bus into a scenic overlook so that we could have a look at a fjord called Kilary Harbor. (A fjord is an inlet with steep sides and deep water.) More interesting to me than the fjord was a strange, permanently-windswept tree with all kinds of debris hanging from it. "That's a fairy tree," Martin said. (Away from his microphone, he didn't stretch out his syllables.) "Leave something of value and the fairies will grant your wish." He explained that fairy trees are always hawthorns, and they get their lopsided, bent-over shape from the wind. It's bad luck to chop a hawthorn tree down, so they are often found in farmers' fields with crops growing all around. I walked closer to the enchanted tree, just behind the scenic view guardrail, and realized that the colorful "junk" hanging from the tree was a collection of socks, handkerchiefs, hats, and a child's rubber

Wellington. All of those people who had been here before me had sacrificed a sock or some trinket to have a chance at a wish being granted. I was traveling light and couldn't think of anything I could spare. Does this mean I can't have my wish? (What would I wish for anyway?)

The hawthorn fairy tree beside the fjord conjured up an image of my own garden at home in New Jersey. I have a lopsided pussy willow tree, its branches next to the house pruned off so as to not disturb the house's siding. It is coincidentally precisely the shape of the fjord's windblown fairy tree. I remember planting the pussy willow myself from a stick given to me by a woman years ago at the public library. (Was that woman a fairy?) A few years ago, before I had any suspicion that my pussy willow was a fairy tree, I strung whimsical solar–powered lights, called FAIRY LIGHTS, on that pussy willow tree. Below it, I placed two tiny store–bought buildings (a fairy house made from a teapot and a wee fairy bakery), a couple of bridges over streams made of blue glass nuggets, shrubs made of magnolia seed pods, and paths made from wood slices, flower pot shards, and clamshells. Fairy gardens have been popular in gardening for the past few years, but who knew if I set one up the fairies would actually inhabit it and sculpt that pussy willow tree to match the fairy trees in Galway?

I'd explored Dublin, Northern Ireland, Tara, Connemara, and Galway and now I was to begin my descent back into my daily routine life. These places steeped in folklore seemed oddly familiar, probably because of the similarity of Grandpa's storytelling style and Mom's long–lost songs. Folktales, storytelling, and song are so much a part of Irish culture that the place seemed familiar from knowing intuitively about its folklore. The places I've described here are the ones I remember best, because they have stories associated with them, either my own or centuries–old tales. But just as with my grandfather's crazy cannibal story, the act of telling the tale or singing the song makes it extraordinary.

I learned about Ireland from its folk songs, legends, and stories. My stories are true, now, but will I be tempted to embellish them in the future? Will I be showered in green bird poo in St. Stephen's Green and live in a 15th–floor dorm room at Trinity College? Will Irish EMTs need to be called to revive me on the hill at Loughcrew shouting "CLEAR!" as the paddles touch my chest? While Irish legends and fairy tales are entertaining and give the visitor an idea of what the Irish find fun, entertaining, and important, they are not to be taken as fact. Even as a child, I didn't believe for one minute that Grandpa's cannibal story had any truth to it, but it was sure fun to hear him tell it.

I intend for my stories to be true. Nonfiction. Not exaggerated. While I seem to have inherited the feel of Irish folk stories from my maternal ancestors, I didn't inherit the gift of embellishment. But how would I know if I did? These biographical stories are true as I recollect them, but can I be sure they haven't been tainted by the stories of other travelers or my own unconscious dreams? My experiences did not actually unfold in a neat sonata–allegro form; my mind imposed that form on my memories and I liked the way it fit. Should I be skeptical about my bits of memoir since discovering this sonata–allegro sleight–of–hand? Please imagine each essay I write with a disclaimer: "The events depicted in this essay are true to the best of my recollection."

Molly Malone, the Hag of Loughcrew, Finn MacCool, and Robin of Galway could have been inspired by real people, I suppose. The stories and songs as we know them, as they were finally recorded, are fanciful. Knowing they aren't true stories doesn't make me cherish them any less. They represent Irish folk culture and provide a shared heritage for the Irish people.

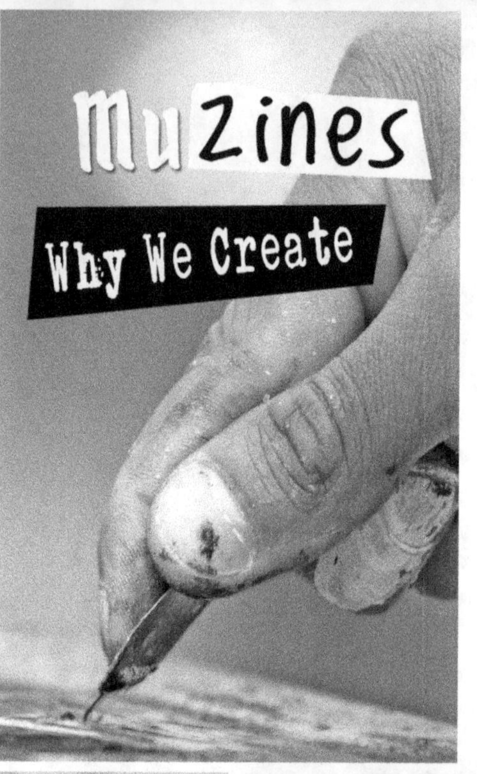

The concept of creation is the idea that we make something out of the void.

But we can do better than that, can't we?

Creation is rebellion from the ordinary...

e purpose of all creative
ts is to make a statement
at is bigger than yourself.
A statement that proclaims
I AM HERE!" with an
dded wave, "Come join
e."

...but it can also be a humble bow to those who have come before us.

We create to know, but we create so we can be known.
What is your rebellion?

–The Hills Above the
McKenzie
–Esalen Hot Springs
–The Yukon Appears
Before Me
–Front Seat Stains

Camden Michael Jones

The Hills above the McKenzie

Younger
I stood on cliff edges
and was light.
I climbed rock walls
to find a breath
in that space between the colors
of the sky.

Younger found footprints
where they shouldn't be,
traced the routes
of homesteaders,
stepped through the envelope
to stay for a time.

The hills above the McKenzie
River flow like the water below,
logging roads cross–stitch
scars under the canopy,
curving over and around
the gold in fairy streams.

Esalen Hot Springs

The cliffs along Big Sur
serpentine the white
tides of the Pacific,
and there is a trail
      paved in the red stone
      that grasps at the heel
      ask to say "Stay"
that descends into a community
called Esalen.

An hour after midnight
we follow our guide's voice
past curtained windows,
fleece–soft in the night,
and step toe–first
into ancient runnings
from a hole in the wall.

The fire within these cliffs
tumbles against the cuneiform
in your feet, whispers past
the wind–rinsed flesh of your ribs,
and settles in that dimple
of your clavicle as the pools
below fill with salt and moonlight.

The Yukon Appears Before Me

Alaskan swamps suck the polish
—black leather
made blacker by wet —
from my loggers,
wool socks damp first
at the arch, then toe,
then in through the hollowed
cavity of my heel
—shallow lakes
around each foot,
turbid particulates
snag in the sea kelp
of my leg hair —

I slide another wound bundle
of inch–and–a–half hose
down the palm–polished
shaft of my Pulaski,
sink another inch,
and squelch—

—squelch down the firebreak
we cut last week through Black
and White Spruce
until the sodden moss
gives way to river bar
—the Yukon appears before me

she (the river, that is),
she carries the aluminum boats
that shouldn't float, sink, sink,
sink full of gated–wyes and nozzles
and miles of hose, and on this
mound of polyester
and river–gray steel
I kneel for the ride.

Front Seat Stains

We came home from vacation
to find the white feathers
of my tom's face
shifted three inches right
and left to pendulum tumble
into the kiddie's pool
where they stood on water and bumped
against the plastic edges.
His chest, once bold / proud / tall
was glued to the sharp grass
with maggots boiling from a gash.

I think he tried jumping: flying:
escaping: over the fence,
only to fall onto the head
of the nail I hung his feed
bucket from. I like to imagine
       he might have said
       It wasn't worth it.

Those avian eyes locked
mine and saw mercy:
in a tarp I placed him
on the front seat
of my '91 Ranger,
drove four miles
into the Oregon desert,
where,

in the headlights
    that made puppet shows
    out of big sagebrush
    and hatchet heads,
I took care of my own.

Part of the Story

Claire Tomasi

I've always loved stories
I can't stop thinking...
I wish I could just, "poof"
run like some magic river,
or some place where no cars go.
would you come with me?

Growing up I struggled greatly with a mental illness I didn't know I had until later in life

I didn't understand it at the time but hours of drawing and writing stories of epic battles, secret worlds, and long lost love paved the way for my dive into the world of my thoughts I wasn't strong enough to face.

Epic fantasy lands and tales of heroes and adventures and love filled my mind with wonder. A welcome relief from the violence of my mind as a young sufferer of suicidal ideation obsessive compulsive disorder

As I grew up, my interest moved from magical fantasy lands to graphic memoir. My mind turned with wanting for a story of my own
Though as I got older, my OCD grew more aggressive.
I tried music and fiction writing as coping mechanism, but my hand ached to draw

And so I began to draw

Psychiatric
It wasn't until my early twenties when my violent obsessions were at their worst

I wanted to take those
thoughts and make
something beautiful instead

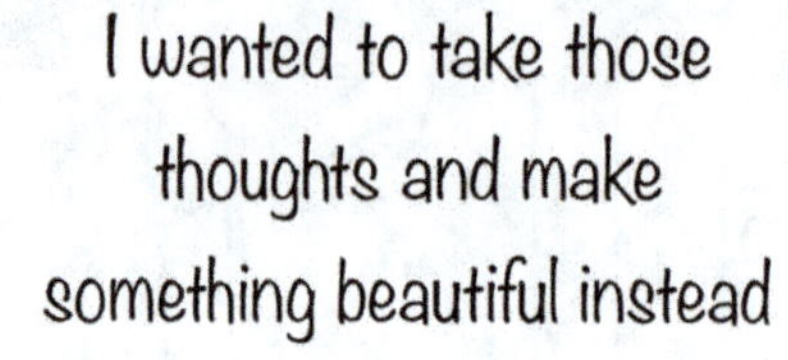

So I read and I wrote comics,

and with the help of therapy, learned to tell my story.

Comics

Though I may struggle with intrusive thoughts from time to time
I know now,

It's just **part** of my story.

A Mother's Tale During COVID-19

Susan Padron

Part One: Before

In the beginning of March, I was a badass business owner. I was in that state that every entrepreneur lives for, where you are just in the flow. Your constant hard work is now visible, you're working with your ideal clients, you feel like there's some kind of balance in your life, and things are just good.

I was also preparing to take my 5 year old son to Disney World for the first time. So, I am not a Disney person. If it weren't for my son, I would have absolutely no desire to be around anything Disney related whatsoever. It's just never been my thing. But, my inlaws offered to take all of us to Disney, and we knew that our little guy would love it.

A few days before we left, I remember my parents asking me, concerned, "Are you guys still going to Disney?"

"Yeah, why? There are no travel restrictions to Florida on the CDC website. We'll wash our hands like responsible adults, and I'm sure we'll be fine." I really didn't think we had any reason to be overly concerned, let alone stay home.

I told my son to be prepared that he may see people wearing masks while we were in the airport, explaining to him that there is a virus, and we have to be extra thorough with washing our hands. So, that's exactly what we did.

We arrived at Disney World on Wednesday, March 11th, and everything seemed normal. We did the things you do at Disney —rides, food, all that Disney stuff.

My sister–in–law and her fiance, who were also on the trip with us, were checking Twitter compulsively for updates. The frequency of their Twitter checks would increase progressively as our trip continued. Their stress induced (also inducing) Twitter scrolling was somewhat valid. By the second day of our trip, Thursday, March 12th, Disney announced that they would be closing the park Sunday night.

That's when shit got real. We changed our flight, so that we could leave Monday morning, instead of Wednesday. Disney added hand sanitizing stations throughout the parks. But, aside from the constant rising cases of COVID–19 being announced all over the world, "The Happiest Place on Earth" remained in its happy bubble, and wow, that felt strange.

Every time a notification went off on my phone, it was a client requesting to cancel, or an event I was invited to host that needed to be rescheduled. Remember that amazing flow state I mentioned earlier? I felt like the wave I was riding was crashing down. I'd say that's probably an accurate time stamp for when my depression started and my anxiety began to climb.

The last night that we were in Disney World, we were leaving Epcot at the end of the night, when the park was closing. This was the last night that Disney World would be open for an unknown length of time. The exit walkway was lined with Disney "cast members" all smiling and waving goodbye to all of us, as we filed out to the monorail and parking lot. I remember thinking, *how many of these people will be affected by this virus? How many of them will get sick, die, or lose a loved one?* Their behavior seemed so normal and "Disney–like." Was it because they wanted to try to spread hope, or were they keeping us in that protective Disney bubble?

We got home from Disney, and I think I was in some combination of shock and denial. My husband and I agreed to keep our son home, even though his school remained open for quite some time. I shifted from badass business working mom, to full time stay-at-home mom, and that shift felt like crashing into a brick fucking wall. I don't remember when exactly, but the initial feelings of shock and denial transitioned quickly into grief. I was mourning the loss of my business, and the freedom from, what felt like, my past life.

Part Two: During

Going from working mom to stay-at-home mom during a quarantine felt very similar to postpartum – you're at home, away from adults, your partner works all day (you used to work all day), and your needs take a back seat to that little human you created. Your emotions are on a roller coaster, and screaming isn't really an option.

Let's take a brief detour to discuss mental health, shall we? For the last 4+ years, I have been on medication to help manage my lifelong battle with anxiety and panic attacks. I have a regular spiritual practice, which includes meditation, sound healing, chakra balancing, energy clearing, journaling, mindfulness, and constant mindset work. I have worked with therapists. I have spiritual mentors. Before the quarantine, I was doing yoga regularly, and receiving both acupuncture and reiki.

I take care of myself.

I consider myself to be adaptable, optimistic, grounded, and strong, but a global trauma is not something anyone could have mentally or emotionally prepared for. Anxiety is being triggered in ways that seem new and old at the same time, and yet, none of my previous skills/tools/etc seem to be doing a damn thing.

Your detour has ended. You may now resume your original route.

I was forced to stop working for multiple reasons. The first reason was for our son's safety. With public schools closing all around us, we wanted to keep him home, despite his private daycare remaining open. The additional reasons happened quickly, so I don't remember the order they occurred, but basically, clients were cancelling, stores were being forced to close, malls shut down, and my business wasn't considered "essential."

Of course, a personal stylist is not essential. I get that. But, it's a strange feeling to hear that your business isn't "essential." I absolutely understand it from a logical perspective, but, when your business receives the unofficial title of "non–essential," it can bring your thoughts to dark places, especially if you are the one who created said business. It's like you and your business both got a huge punch in the emotional gut.

So, what did I do? I stopped. I stopped trying to work, to create, and I tried to be the best stay-at-home mom that I could be. You better believe I made a homeschool schedule that included school work, creative play time, outside time, and whatever else I'm sure you saw on those pictures that your friends posted on social media of the schedules they created for their kids.

And that lasted for a couple of weeks. What happened was, eventually, both my son and I hated the schedule. I was bored with it, and I knew that if I disliked it that much, my little guy hated it even more. I would go to bed at night, anxious about the next day. My nerves were fried. I felt resentful towards my husband, because he was still working, and thus able to leave the house, have his own thoughts, make decisions for himself, and listen to podcasts (oh, how I missed podcasts). I immediately felt guilty about having any kind of resentment towards my husband, because he really is an incredible human and partner, and then I became worried for his safety. And then I felt like an asshole. So, I cried a lot, and knew that something about my daily life had to change.

Part Three: During, but Later

My friend and fellow creative, Stacey Fay, sent me a message pretty early on in the quarantine, telling me that she had an idea, and asked if we could chat on Zoom about it. She gave me a brief description of her idea, and I eagerly awaited our call. This call resulted in the birth of our video series and podcast,

"The Creative Pause."

Up until this moment, I had been dealing with only uncertainty both in my business and my life. So when Stacey suggested creating something together, it felt like we were being guided to help people (and ourselves) in a way that we all desperately needed. It was crucial for us to provide a space for people to connect, whether the connection was literal, by joining in the show live, or emotional through a connection with what was shared in the show. The other key element to "The Creative Pause" involved encouraging our audience to take a little bit of time each day to do something that brings them joy. Connection and joy were two of the main pieces that both Stacey and I were missing in our lives. We needed it just as much as we wanted to provide it for our audience.

So many of our guests on "The Creative Pause" shared the message that there is beauty through imperfection, especially when you are in the creative process. I don't know that I ever really connected with being a perfectionist, but what I realized is that the fear of imperfection prevented me from trying a lot of new things. Hearing the message of "beauty through imperfection" over and over again eventually guided me to doing things like flower pressing, watercolor painting, lettering, cooking, baking, and establishing deeper connections with myself, nature, and my spirituality.

I am still trying to see all of the lessons that I have learned from being in quarantine; what are the elements of my new life that I am looking forward to taking with me, when our days have more flexibility?

I want to continue to support small and local businesses over big businesses, but no longer from a fear that they need my support, but because I want to help. I want to make the time to be able to prepare and cook the majority of our family meals, so we can be nourished with good food and love. Cooking has also become a creative outlet, and I would like to continue to create in the other ways that I have incorporated into my life. Quality alone time is something that I need to function at my best self. Spending time being surrounded by nature is also a necessity for me to recharge. These are beyond self care for me, it's what I need to help my mental health. At the same time, I need quality time being present with those I love.

Thinking about the future still makes me anxious. All of the unknowns and uncertainty stress me out, for sure. I'm going to try to shift my focus away from fear. I want to bring joy and connection to my life every day, and continue to help others find it too.

An Afternoon in
the Life

Carolyn Banks

muzines

There's writing on the landscape, they say. It's all in how you decipher it.

houlder to shoulder with
he archetypes of every day
ife, each one a multitude in
ts own right.

he circle perpetuates itself
nd becomes routine,
mundane.
The fog on the horizon.

It's all commonplace...
until the moment
it is not.

Angry Couplets to the Red Queen

Elliott Stegall, PhD.

Furious Lit

I don't know who you are. You've taken things too far.
You know you've come undone. You've hurt everyone.
Taste of blood in your mouth. Wicked witch of the South.
Do you feel proud Acting out so loud?
Showing off to your crowd Glowing red in your shroud?
And what have you gained? Your heart is stained Forever and
ever.
And never again will you be innocent. The pain in your soul
will be heaven–sent.
Your children will fear you Now that they hear you
And see what you've done, Your daughter and son
Know you've murdered their father
They'll never forgive you, so why even bother
Your plan went off with nary a hitch. Now everyone knows
that you're a mean …snitch
Did you ever really love? Did you think of God above?
Did you even stop to think? Just how low will you sink?
This time, It's a true crime. You've killed a good man. Do you
even understand
What you've done? Your madness blots out the sun.
Something's wrong with your head. You'd rather hate instead.
You won't listen to reason. Your mind's all out of season.
You won't hear my prayer. You won't even share
A moment or two of affection. Your lips are a rotten
confection
Dripping with disdain Perpetuating pain.

Your smile used to cover a mile. Now it hides your denial.
Your eyes used to light up the sky. Now they make angels cry.
You're so good at faking it. You think that you're making it.
The hatred in you Will catch up to you.
Is a scorched earth All that you're worth?

Burning all in your path Because of your wrath.
Over what? A minor cut. Let there be healing. You can stop this mad reeling.
You could let him back in. Learn to love him again.
You can forgive sin. It's the only way to win.
But we all know you. We know what you do.
You'd rather stab out your eyes Than apologize.
Even when you know you're right. You are better than this and you might
Even make a new start Heal a broken heart. Or two. Yes, me and you.
But you just can't seem to hide Your spiteful and mean pride.
Someday you too will falter. Only love from you can halt her.
That raving mad queen The one that you've seen In the mirror each day, As the years tick away
staring back at you, filled with rue.
And who will be there to hold When you get sick and old?
You used to be so bold. Winter's coming you soon will be cold.
It's running faster than you understand. The reaper's alabaster hand
Is already reaching. Listen! You can hear him screeching Both day and night. You'd better get your soul right The end is in sight.
So you've made your own bed, And you've filled it with dread Go and sleep in it. Are you keeping it just for you? Is there someone else there too?
Is there someone else in you? The red queen and you. The killer inside. You know that she lied.
There's no love anymore. You locked the door To keep him away. And in your trap Alone you'll stay.
You've finally done it. The battle has run and you've won it.

Furious Lit

You've brought down your king, And he'll no longer sing
you a love song named for you. Your family is broken, and
you are too
So don't take the blame for the evil you do. It's still such a
shame, and the blood is on you.

Grandead

Matt Lydon

"So you wore her pink bathrobe into the street, got into your car and drove back home? How did you get your wallet back?" Bill McGonigle asked his friend Connor MacGruber, as he took a healthy slug from his beer.

MacGruber, or Mac, as he was better known among his friends, smiled and turned toward his own beer, raising it slowly to his lips as a smile spread across his face. Mac continued, "Well, a week later, I get a manila envelope with my wallet inside, missing 100 bucks, and a note that said, 'Thanks, Mac, for the good time and for the new bathrobe. You owed me.' I certainly did, and she was welcome to it. Her husband is still none the wiser, and I see him every day at work to this day!" Bill laughed, said cheers and raised his glass to Mac.

Not everybody was so keen on this story, though, "Bullshit, Mac. You're a goddamn liar!"

Immediately to the right of Mac, hunched over his own pint, was the third man of this trio: Anthony Merkowski, or Merk, for short. Merk was a short, tubby guy, his hair patchy in places, and his beard shot through with more salt than pepper. Of the three men, he was always the guy calling your bluff, keeping you honest, and making sure you paid your fair share when the time came to settle up the tab. He was also, because of all this, sometimes an insufferable asshole. But Bill and Mac were already so far into their cups, they just laughed at Merk. Mac stopped laughing long enough to say, "Oh yeah, Merk? You're just jealous because you couldn't do the same as me!"

Merk turned toward Mac, and the look on Merk's

face sobered up Mac and Bill next to him, quickly. "You know my Cindy is better looking than Ed Kowalski's Janet, any day. And if you're impugning my manhood, we can take this into the street for a donnybrook if you're game. How about it, Mac?"

Mac gulped, and politely declined, but didn't stop there. "Fine, you're right. But Merk, remember: you're up. I told a story, Bill told a story, now YOU tell a story! It's the rules, and winner doesn't chip in for the tab tonight." Mac was correct. His own story of marital infidelity was currently in the lead for winner of the night over Bill's story of getting his tongue frozen to a bus stop sign while he waited for the 66 bus to come take him to work one bitterly cold February morning. Merk was indeed next in the queue, and if he forfeited, Mac would drink free tonight.

"When you're right, you're right. I've been wracking my brain to find a story I haven't told you all that might put me in the winner's circle. I don't think I have one," said Merk. Mac whooped loudly, and started to call to Crane, the bartender, to grab him a Chimay off the premium shelf.

Suddenly, Mac felt the weight of a solidly built hand pressing on the front of his work shirt. "Not so fast, Mac. I've got at least five minutes to come up with said story, yeah?"

Merk looked at Bill, who nodded assent, and back at Mac, who agreed that was the case. "Yeah, Merk, Five minutes, but not a second longer. I'm timing you, but Crane, don't let the Chimay go too far!" Mac fished his pocket watch out of his pocket, and scanned the face until the second hand crossed the twelve. "Time starts NOW!"

Merk looked down into his beer, and smiled as he sipped from his pint glass. Bill and Mac looked on, counting seconds under their breath. Two minutes stretched to 3 and a half minutes, and Mac could almost taste the pure freedom of gratis alcohol as the seconds ran out on Merk's hourglass. Merk, for his part, was completely nonplussed, and looked at his two friends, winked, and slammed the rest of his beer. He cleared his throat, turning to Mac and Bill and said, "Here goes. A true ghost story starring my father."

Bill's eyes widened and he actually yelped, "Yes! Let's hear it!" while Mac, on the other hand, cursed Merk under his breath.

"You fellas know my old man was a complete bastard, yeah?" Merk began. "Drank a ton, yelled at my mom, and threatened my brother and me. He was such an asshole, but for all his threats, he never actually got physical. Thanks for being a huge prick, Dad," said Merk.

Mac rolled his eyes, and Bill looked away a bit nervously. Was this story going to get more entertaining? They wondered. The bartender Crane walked by, and Merk signaled for another beer. Seemingly seconds later, a fresh lager slid into Merk's open hand, at which he nodded his thanks to Crane, who was already down at the other end of the bar, tending to other patrons.

Merk continued:

"Anyway, the old bastard eventually got cancer,

or cirrhosis of the liver, or something equally painful and fatal. Maybe it was both. Anyway, his yelling continued unabated, his threats to me and my brother never went away, but he stopped yelling at my mother. Probably because he needed her, the sicker he got. He was so sick and weak, she had to roll him over out of bed. Helped him shower and all that. Just weak and pathetic and terrible." Here, Merk stopped for a long pull from his pint glass. Mac thought to himself if the story doesn't get better than this, he might just kill himself rather than try to survive for the free alcohol that surely awaited after this bummer of a story.

Still, Merk is undaunted, "Like I said, as my father is deteriorating, he's still yelling at me and Jake, but now there's a smell in the house. I didn't know what it was at the time, but I would come to know that smell as the one that comes on folks who are on their way out. Call it flop sweat, or death bed sweat if you want, but it's a real thing that happens to us all. So, this flop sweat/death bed sweat is increasing each day, as are his yells for Jake and I to get jobs since he's dying. Jake made the mistake of saying Dad kind of smelled, and somewhere, Dad marshalled the wherewithal to throw a bedpan at him that HAD actually been used within the last 48 hours. Used but not emptied," he said, then took another swig.

"Ew, Merk. You can't be serious!" Merk looked at Bill, the look on his face clarifying that Merk was, in fact, serious.

"Anyway," Merk continued, "Dad used to love this terrible cologne back in the angular black bottle, with a name that sounded almost Swedish, like–

"Drakkar Noir!" yelled Bill. Merk raised an eyebrow and paused, Bill understood the question. "My older brother Petey was a huge fan. Claimed it drove the girls wild," Bill offered.

"And did it?"Mac asked, genuinely curious.

"I mean… I can't remember seeing Petey ever bring a girl home, now that you think about it. He'd mostly just bring his friend David for sleepovers and they'd go fishing early the next morning," Bill finished. Merk and Mac looked at each other, nodded, and smirked.

"What, you guys? You never go fishing with your best friend?"

Mac's smirk was in danger of becoming laughter, but Merk cut it off. "No, no. Sure I have. Just… not with a sleepover the night before. How bout you, Mac?"

Mac shook his head vigorously to keep quiet.

"What are you guys saying, Merk?" Bill wondered out loud. Merk never met Petey, nor had Mac, but if Bill couldn't recognize there might be a secret about his older brother, then neither man was going to be the first to tell him.

"As I was saying, though," Merk re–entered his story to alleviate the creeping cognitive dissonance in Bill's brain, "Dad loved that stuff, and thought it smelled great. My mother, brother and I thought otherwise. Given the choice in front of us, though, between dad's flop sweat and Drakkar? We chose the Drakkar." Merk punctuated the sentence with another slug of his beer.

"A few months later, I'm at school and Dad passes

away. I was called to the office over the PA system, and I go down to see the principal. Principal was an Archdiocesan priest who wasn't too great with people. He stood behind his desk, and tried to say something encouraging, or at least intelligible, but just couldn't get it out. Father Simmons, that was the name. Anyway, Simmons comes around, puts a sweaty hand on my shoulder and says, 'It'll be okay, son. Don't you worry. Trust in God.' Me, I just shrugged and asked him if I could go. His mouth hit the floor, but he shook his head and said, 'Yes, I guess so. We'll offer up intentions for your family at mass this Sunday.' And I just walked back to chemistry, but stopped off in the bathroom for a smoke." Merk drained the last of his beer and smacked the empty pint glass down on the soggy coaster in front of him.

Bill and Mac started to chuckle. "Amusing, for sure, Merk," Mac began, "but tab–worthy? I don't know, what do you think, Bill?" Shaking his head and laughing, Bill agreed it didn't quite measure up to Mac's story, even though it was better than his own story about his frozen tongue.

"Mac's right, Merk. And you never even got to the ghost! I think that you and me have to—"

"Hold it right there, boys. I wasn't finished," Merk said. Another signal to Crane at the other end of the bar, another pint slid down into Merk's open hand, and a long sip later, Merk started up again. "So a year later, I graduate and move out. Couple years after that, my brother does the same, leaving Mom behind in that house by herself. She finally gets to breathe without the old man around, starts going out with friends, playing Bingo down at the church hall, gets a dog. The whole nine yards. She's happy, and even though my old man was a pure bastard to her, she misses him. The weird thing? She only mentions missing him when she's drunk on krupnik or nalewki down at the Polish league with her girlfriends. Otherwise, she referred to him as her 'was–band'."

Merk paused there again, to take another sip. In the silence, Bill pipes up. "OOOoooh. Was–band. Like, husband, but was, like in past–tense!" Mac almost chokes on laughter, turns to Bill and punches him in the arm, yelling, "Geezus, man, you're an idiot. You sure you're Irish, and not like —?"

From the other end of the bar, Crane the barkeep yells, "Hey, what the fuck have I told you about using that word in here? I'll toss you out on your ass, Mac!" Merk rolls his eyes at Mac, as does Bill. Mac hangs his head in shame, because he remembers Crane telling them about his daughter Olivia, a sweet girl with special needs. Kids at her school were cruel, and that word made her cry, so Crane wanted to eliminate it from his own vocabulary, as well as from the vernacular of his environment. A smaller man might not have successfully done this at a corner bar in a working class neighborhood, but Crane was not only his surname, but a pretty fair description for the size and strength of the man. Never mind how easily he could pick up offenders of the bar's rules and eject them at a moment's notice. "Sorry, Crane, "mumbles Mac, "really my bad. Won't happen again."

"See that it doesn't. Another beer?" Crane was good at chastising his patrons, but also anticipating their alcoholic needs. It was a balancing act, like most of Crane's life. When he was a kid, he couldn't sit still or stop talking and his parents were always yelling at him to shut up. Back then, he was Jimmy Crane the Super Sonic Plane. Until he reached high school. As a freshman, his hyperactivity and constant talking gathered people to him who wanted to hear what was going to come out of this skinny kid's motor mouth next. It was entertaining to most, except for some upperclassmen who honestly just wished he'd shut up. After school one day, several of the guys from the shop class followed Jimmy Crane to the bathroom and upended him, dousing him headfirst into the toilet. "That'll teach ya to shut up, huh freshman?" the flannel shirt crew catcalled at Jimmy. Not a particularly original bit of delinquency, but Jimmy's small arms couldn't push back from the porcelain to keep the fetid water of the restroom out of his nose and mouth. With so much water splashing into his airways, he passed out and went limp, which caused the flannel shirts and carpenter jeans to scatter. When he came to later on, coughing and spluttering, he vowed never to be overpowered like that again.

Jimmy diverted his hyper energy from his mouth and peripatetic movements into a weight training program and by junior year was so solidly packed with muscle the teachers and peers all called him Jim Crane the Amtrak Train. At junior prom, he confronted the flannel shirt crew again, as most of them failed and had been left back more than once. Their dull eyes looked up at him over their cups of punch, their faces flooding with fear. He put his now huge hands on the shoulders of the nearest of the crew, and bent down to look directly into a shaky boy's eyes. He hadn't even said anything before he smelled a wet, ammoniac smell. Looking down, the boy had had an accident that was pooling towards Jimmy's shoes. Still, this caused Jimmy to pause. What he saw in the face of that kid that day changed his mind about needing revenge. The weak and powerless are often driven to find someone, something, anything they can dominate to make themselves feel larger. Jimmy Crane looked at the kid, and around the circle at all his friends, and said, "You have a good night." Then walked away. Realizing his own power, Jimmy Crane vowed he'd never raise a hand to someone unless he needed to defend someone who couldn't defend themselves. That night, he was no longer Jim Crane the Amtrak Train, but simply Crane. He often wondered if he should tell that story some night at the bar, but that was Jimmy Crane the Super Sonic Plane's territory. He was fine just being Crane.

"Crane?" Mac shook his empty pint glass at Crane, who'd already pulled a fresh pint in his reverie. Crane shook his head a bit to clear the mist of memory from his conscious mind, then walked the beer from the tap and handed it off to Mac, asking Merk, "I believe you were in the middle of telling a story, yes?" Merk nodded, and continued.

"So, I get married, have kids, my brother does the same. Mom loves being a grandma, spoils all our kids rotten. She's getting older, and frailer, so she starts staying at my place for a week, then at Jake's. The kids love having their grandma around, and to be honest, I did, too. Then she gets sick.

Worst news: lung cancer. Inoperable. Stage IV. Seems Mom took up smoking with the girls down at the Polish league." Bill and Mac's faces purse and they mumble a few *geezes* and *sorry–to–hear–that's*. Merk presses on. "When Mom did something, she did it big. This was no exception. So yeah, she starts dying, slowly. So slowly in fact, it almost seems like she's getting better. Keeps shuffling around from my house to my brother's house and her sister's in Juniata. But, she took a fall and broke her ankle, so she was confined at her own house for a while. I was staying with her, when the weirdest thing happened." Merk looks into the faces of both of his friends, who are hanging on each word now. "I start to smell Drakkar Noir in the house."

The boys erupt. "What do you mean? Is she spraying it around the house? What gives?" Merk smiles and shakes his head. "No! I hated that shit! It's only Old Spice deodorant for me, pal. But no, Mom isn't spraying it around the house. She's kind of confined to bed on the broken ankle. But there it is, unmistakable: Drakkar Noir in her house, like it's 1988 and I'm back in junior year of high school."

Mac and Bill shake their heads and take slurps from their beers, indicating Merk should go on. "I wake up the next morning, and my mom is gone. Not in her room, not down in the kitchen or the basement. Gone. Even her car, that old Lincoln town car she and dad bought in the 70s, is gone."

Mac asks, "So, where did she go, Merk?"

"Turns out, Mom hobbled down to her car that

morning about 5am, drove over to her sister's, my Aunt Kate's, and holes up there for a while. I call around and finally get that news from Kate. I ask her why the hell did she leave. Aunt Kate says, 'you better hear this from her. Ang!" So she hands my mother the phone, and I ask her, 'Ma, why did you leave on a broken ankle?' She says to me: 'it was your father.' I say, are you drunk? Dad's been dead like 20 years! She says, 'Anthony, I'm not drunk at all, but this morning, your father was in my room, putzing around looking for his glasses or some god–forsaken thing so he could see me better or something. Told me to wait until he found them, and we could leave together. I said no way, and went down to the car and came to Katie's. He never liked Katie and so far, hasn't followed me here!'"

Bill and Mac are now falling about the place, laughing. "Your mom was serious? Thinks she's seeing your dad?"

Merk nods and smiles. "The next month or so, we sell her car because she's not driving it anymore. Mom bounces back between my house, Jake's, Aunt Kate's and the doctors. Pain gets so bad, they prescribe an IV drip, but she doesn't want to go home. But then, one day, she's sitting on my couch, watching Judge Judy, and she turns to me and says, 'Anthony, I think I'm ready for your father now. You can take me home tomorrow.' So, I get her all packed up, and we drive her over in my car. Open the door, and the house is pretty much like I'd left it a month before, except now, no Drakkar Noir smell."

Mac interrupts, "So no ghost, huh? That's a

relief!"

Merk puts a hand up. "Hold on."

The boys look at Merk as he turns to take another swig from his beer, and notice that Merk's bottom lip is trembling a bit, and that his eyes seem glassy, a bit wet, almost as if he's on the verge of tears. Neither of them say anything, but lean in so Merk can finish his story. "I stay the night, just to make sure my mom's going to be okay. About 3 am, I get woken up. Mom's calling from the other room. Not like, in a panic or anything, just kind of like, 'Anthony, come here please.' So I go. She's lying there in her bed, exhausted, but a smile on her face and I ask her what's going on. She calls me closer, and I ask her again, ma, what's going on? She touches my face, and says, 'I just wanted you to know that you and Jacob have been the best sons a girl like me could ask for. Always remember that, kiddo,' I told her I would, and that she should rest. I tucked her in, and said good night. She says, 'Same to you. Oh, leave the hall light on for your father, would you?' I turned it on and laughed to myself a little bit, but as I flicked that switch... I smelled Drakkar again!"

"No way!" the boys say in unison.

Merk nods vociferously. "I know, right? So, next morning, I sleep through my alarm, but it's warm, birds and chirping outside, the whole bit. I go in to check on Mom and—" Merk paused here and this time, Bill and Mac were sure of it, his lower lip did tremble and a single tear fell from his eye. A sharp intake of breath, and a hand from either man on his shoulder later, Merk was able to continue. "She'd passed. She was cold. She was gone, but still, that smile on her face. I bent down to kiss her forehead before I went to call my wife and tell her the sad news. As I did, there was that damn smell of Drakkar again. I'd started crying, but laughed at that stupid cologne. I turned my head to the nightstand as I braced myself to stand back up, and I saw a note. Picked it up, and it read, 'Thanks for looking out for her, meathead. You and your idiot brother were good for something. Dad.'

Merk nodded, and as a finishing flourish, took down the rest of his beer in one long draught. Mac, Bill and now even Crane had leaned in from their various positions around the bar, and were agog. None of the men spoke, and the only thing heard in the background was the hum of the bar stereo and a rerun of Judge Judy playing on the TV screen above the bar.

The quiet between the men was full of something, though what that was, none of the men there could have said. It wasn't awkward, necessarily, but something had been adjusted in the atmosphere that made for an air of difference, of otherness.

A sweet chill, a tingle that started at the base of each man's spine radiated quickly upward and outward, making each man shudder in turn. Not a shudder in horror, but the shudder that the living get when they are in the presence of things you can't explain or prove, but know to be true. Bill started to speak, but Crane and Mac put a finger to their lips to prolong the silence. Bill understood immediately and quieted back down. At least, for another 30 seconds.

"Holy shit, Merk! You just blew my mind! Mac, we definitely have to—" Bill's lips were stopped by a large, powerful finger. Crane had leaned over the bar to button Bill's lip for him. The large barman shook his head and stared Bill back into quietus, but picked up where Bill had left off. "Yes, we definitely have to pick up your tab tonight, Merk. But gents, all three of your tabs are on me tonight. Even you, Mac. Just don't get used to it."

Usually, something like this would cause all three men, Mac, Bill, and Merk, to cheer, but instead the four men leaned in that much closer to the bar, and clasped each other in a close, warm, awkward hug. The three friends noticed it was about midnight, and since it was a work night, they started to settle up but since Crane had zeroed out their tabs, each man just put a twenty dollar bill on the bar rail for him. Mac got his jacket on first, and shuffled out the door, with Bill just behind him, looking for his bus pass. Merk stood up, shook Crane's hand, and grabbed his own coat off the hook by the door of the bar.

As Merk stepped out the door onto the sidewalk and began his walk home, his nose began to run in the winter cold. He wiped away as best he could, and sniffed sharply inward, but it wasn't the cold, or the mucus, or the fried foods from Crane's bar that caressed Merk's olfactory nerves. It was the 1980s odor of Drakkar Noir.

He continued walking home in the midnight chill. "Damn you, dad."

–Ode to Expressive Aphasia
–Yes, a Wanderer's Yes
–Fish & Game Code:
Division 6. Part 1 Chapter
7. Amphibia Article 2. 6883

Jo Freehand

Ode to Expressive Aphasia

*Oh horror, horror, horror! Tongue nor heart cannot conceive nor
name thee! Confusion now hath made his masterpiece!*

–Shakespeare, "Macbeth"

Trickster, you trickster, oh how you humor me,
oh how you make me work for normalcy.
We have laughed, haven't we? Maybe not
during one of our two–hour–on–one–sentence
gatherings.
Without you, how could I so thoroughly inhabit two
words
and then, as thoroughly, inhabit the next?
Our private game of Spit–It–Out requires two
players,
ages … ages what? How long?
How long have we been together Aphasia,
you and I close as my left frontal lobe, close as a brain
injury,
close as a family portrait etched deep upon my cortex,
portrait in gilded frame hanging in well–lit hall of
right hemisphere.
Aphasia, you are close as that blown circuit in the
gallery across the way,
velvet roped–off Broca's Area, Regions 44 and 45.
It's unspeakable, you and I in the dark. I won't tell,
darling you know you drive me to the edge of
comprehension.
Who would I tell? You have taught me to listen and
divert.

For you I dance. For you I paint.
Have I ever embraced you the way you deserve to be
embraced?
Even you, Aphasia, deserve to be Aphasia. That I can
now say.
Masterful abstract expressionist with little regard for
detail,
Your skillful brush brings me halt, I wait in silence.
I realize essence without sequence.
I want order. I know better.
I want to hear it. I want to speak it. I want to write it.
I know better.
You're right, there was a time when I needed us.
You're right, I came to you first.
Remember the howling? Remember calling out for our
mother?
Remember cement–kneeling for Mercy?
Remember our week–long silent retreat in the children's
ward?
Remember how we refused to say –it wasn't the cat that
got our tongue.

Yes, a Wanderer's Yes

Comes with a roar
comes with a whisper,
comes with a sigh,
this Yes, and this Yes
leaves the door open,
blows farewell kiss to
how? why? but what about?
but do you know that you are _______?
Invisible yet tangible Yes
says yes and yes and
yes and yes.
Makes something out of nothing,
this Wanderer's Yes, air in motion,
propelling forward, propels on,
this Yes, creator of lift,
Fool, foot on the edge, ready,
Yes, a tunic catching wind,
Yes, keeper of vessels afloat,
Yes, mover of stagnant waters,
Yes, carrying prayers and pollen,
Without Yes, a most uninhabitable world,
Yes, gust of benediction,
Yes, a god breathing life into clay,
Yes, a sculptor of lands,
Yes, lifting language into poem.
Yes, whorls and flows in a desert,
Yes, shape–shifter, clouds to dragons,
humans more human,
Yes, changer of course,
Yes, meandering Yes

Fish & Game Code: Division 6.
Part 1. Chapter 7. Amphibia
Article 2. 6883

It's illegal to eat a frog
that dies during a frog jumping contest
–or use it for any other purpose–
in California.
It's against Calaveras County Fair rules to touch it
once it's on the starting lily,
you can sing any song you wish
or leap any way you leap
frog leap frog leap leap frog frog frog leap
dance any way you dance, whistle any way you
whistle
or stomp or yell or blow to get your frog to begin,
to crave trophy, to straight line it from center of pad
to as far as possible without tripping
into frog jockey or jockey's equipment.
You can train a frog, says so on
the County Fair home page.
Thanks to Mark Twain, frogs at least 4" nose to tail,
have spent time at the pre–competition Frog Spa
for almost a hundred years.
I don't have plans to go to Frogtown,
not at this point, not because you must agree
to be photographed with your frog,
although there was a time when I couldn't imagine
my frog being so visible, visible at all.

I might change my mind come August.
It's just that, right now, I don't think I want to force
my frog to jump in a straight line or to be so mea-
sured.
Nor do I want to stand behind it
and shout or heavy boot–it along or
lunge at it head–first to trigger flight.
I don't want to do that to my frog.
My frog is a rebellious please–no–labels sort
that would dare you to devour it or bite by bite it.
Most of the time I'm not even certain
that what I have is a frog. Others have questioned
the same.
But if it is, I think I'll let my frog go
in a circle, if a circle is where it wants to go.
Remember, it's illegal to eat a frog
that dies during a frog jumping contest
in California.

A Bundle of Joy

Candice Lola

The Crazy Guy on the Train is yelling out mean things about Women.

He is yelling out really mean things about Black Women.

Hey, you just came from church? You Stupid Black Bitches don't believe in God, you don't even believe in God, do you? You just believe in dick and you gone make yo daughter believe in dick and you gone run some Poor Mothafugga down and make him a Little Bitch too. Tugh!

The Stupid Black Bitch he is spewing this at puts her earbuds in Her Daughter's ears and turns on something loud and distracting, and then stares directly ahead at the passing buildings and streets. Her Daughter giggles at something on her phone screen and I can't help but wish I were six again.

The man sitting a section away leans forward in a way that lets you know that his headphones aren't all the way turned up, which lets you know that maybe he feels some responsibility for Stupid Black Bitch and Her Daughter, or maybe he is just nosey.

Before he got on the train Crazy Guy was running from Angry Middle Eastern Store Owner, and before that he was masturbating in an alley, and before that he was cursing out Stupid Black Bitch who wouldn't look at him, and before that he was trying to stop her from walking past because it had been awhile since he had gotten any.

Before that he was inside his friend's house, laying on the couch watching a blaxploitation movie from the 70's, and before that his Friend's Girlfriend stormed out of the house after finding out her boyfriend has cheated on her again, and right after that she called him a fucking Ignorant No Good Nigga as he laid on the couch.

Before that he'd smoked a blunt to calm his nerves, and before that he was talking a walk outside because the day was gorgeous, and during that walk a Police Officer (fucking PIG) pushed him into a wall, because just before that he told him that he didn't have any ID.

Before that he was with his Niggas, who bullied two Dyke Bitches who tried to avoid them.

Years before that he was a High School Dropout, because before that he picked up more hours at his grocery store job because His Mom needed him to, because before that His Father said you are The Man of the House and the Police Officers (fucking PIGS) lugged him away, because before then he was a Common Drug Dealer because before then he'd found out that Grandma was about to lose her house, and didn't know of another way to raise money she needed.

Before that Grandma was fired, because before that she had celebrated her 65th birthday. The cake was too dry because while it was baking Grandma was yelling at Slutty 12 Year Old Sister for her jeans being too tight. Before that her Protective Brother had told Grandma that she needed to talk to her Fast Ass, because before then his friends had told him about how much they walked to fuck her.

His Fast Ass Sister had asked one of them for help at the grocery store because she had to use food stamps to buy the food for the party, which she felt ashamed about because earlier a girl at school she didn't know had called her a Lazy Welfare Hoe.

Before then she had asked Her Brother if he wanted to watch TV with her, to which he replied no because he doesn't watch bitch dramas, because long before then he was called Gay by his cousin for laughing at Golden Girls with his Grandma, and then his cousin punched him so that he knew it was an insult, thankfully, because before then he had never heard the word before.

Before then his Mother had been around and he'd spend a lot of time with her, because before then he had trouble adapting His Teacher said, he seems to have trouble talking to other children, because before then a boy had called him The N–Word and then punched him so that he knew it was an insult, and so he punched back.

His Mother went up to the school and talked about how That White Boy called My Baby Nigger and then My Baby is the one that has the problem?? And took his hand and stormed out when she found out that That White Boy was going to be in school the next day, and that The Principal (fucking Uncle Tom) would not divulge his punishment.

Before that he had loved school, back when he was a Boy With Promise, look how fast he can run His Father would say, and His Mom would say what about Your Daughter and His Father would say humph, just make sure she grow up right.

He didn't run anymore except for away, because before then he and His Father had a fight, because before then he was caught wearing His Mother's jacket and skirt because holding them was not enough anymore. She was gone, because before then she had caught Her Husband cheating for the umpteenth time, because before then His Boys had called him a Whipped Bitch when he'd first rejected Some Hoe's advances.

I'm a Man what the fuck do you expect, if you leave you will never see Your Kids again and then he made sure of it, he was very determined, because long before that His Father told him they always come back for the money and the kids.

She didn't get a chance to, because before she could she died, because before she had gotten into her car that day The Girl That Killed Her was drinking, because before then her cousin had called her a Slut because of a vicious rumor Some Asshole spread because before that His Friends called him a Virgin Nerd.

The family never found out that Mom had died in an accident, because before that she had lost her wallet, because before that she had been crying and was too distraught to search for it.

So when His Son wore His Mother's dress it ruined His Father, who yelled stop that shit you ain't no bitch, or are you, maybe you are a Little Bitch because he looked like he was about to cry.

That Trick Left Us, man the fuck up about it, because before that the Little Bitch had been crying and crying and asking for His Mom that he never heard from, sobbing into the skirt that hung from his waist

because

before he was a Crazy Guy on the Train,
or a High School Dropout,
or a Man Of The House,
or a Protective Brother,
or a Gay,
or an N–word,
or a Nigger,
or a Boy With Promise,
or a Little Bitch
he was just Max
he was just a Boy
he was just a Bundle Of Joy in His Mother's Arms.

Prometheus Forgot His Phone

Samantha Atzeni

When it's time to discuss a reading in class, I tell my students that we must "gather around the fire." It is equal parts an attempt to spark our primal, storytelling instinct and lightening the guaranteed freshman panic that comes with the first college seminar. I mime picking up a heavy piece of firewood and throwing it into the center of the room, stoking the flames of inspiration. Some students roll their eyes - it's just another eccentric, batty professor - and some get into the silliness and help me "gather" firewood. Once we decide the flames are cozy enough, we begin discussing our story.

For fifteen weeks, twice or maybe once a week, we sit together and try to bring the real world, at times a scary and foreboding place, into our classroom. We live in a world where a cell phone vibration might mean a text message or an alert that something has happened on campus or in our community. I can't keep this away from them or from myself. So, we tell each other stories. We talk about imaginary characters as a softened lens to the harsh world waiting for us beyond our classroom doors. For however long we're together, we discuss stories that we've read or experienced or heard from others.

Sometimes we talk about living through trauma, struggling against authoritative norms, or navigating social cues.

Sometimes we talk about our weekends.

Sometimes we talk about those weird personality

nuances - the ones you think at nineteen make you different, but really make you hopelessly and wonderfully ordinary.

Sometimes we talk over our time.

Sometimes we run out of things to say.

Sometimes we leave with more questions.

For fifteen weeks, we are a core group of learners - no more than 20.

For fifteen weeks, we work together to write and to share ideas.

For fifteen weeks, I see these students in my classroom...and sometimes speak to them every day via email, office hours, or on campus.

For fifteen weeks, we are an integral part of each other's landscape. Our little community becomes a staple to the larger campus backdrop. There's a comfort there - I will always be in my office on Friday afternoons and they will also be at their desks when it's time for class to begin. This is an unspoken rule agreed upon long before any of us set foot on this campus.

Unfortunately, I don't know what happens when they leave the room, collecting their things in a flurry of activity and yelling goodbye to me over their shoulders. I don't know where they end up after our semester together. Students graduate, transfer, drop out, change majors - or in the extreme cases, they die.

In my twelve years teaching as an adjunct professor, I have said goodbye to seven students. I never intended to say these goodbyes; in fact, I took for granted that their entire lives were ahead of them. I allowed myself to be tricked into the idea that life follows the same pattern for all of us. I forgot about the hidden dark corners of the world, the ones that enjoy reminding us how fragile and vulnerable we truly are.

I have comforted the friends they leave behind, I have attended memorials, I have cried for them, these souls that we lose. I cry mostly for their lost futures - the lost potential that comes with a life gone too soon. Other times, I cry because of that disappointment that comes with false expectations. I expect them to achieve greatness when they leave my classroom. I expect them to be extraordinary. Seeing their names in a "loss in our community" email ends the story that I've made for them. At nineteen, you think you've seen it all, but you are still early in your first act. I cry for the missing narrative points that they will miss. I cry because I was selfish and I believed my story for them was the one that would stick.

We don't know each other as well as we think we do. They see me as their dodgy old professor, when in fact I was just slightly older than them when I began teaching. I lied about my age so I wouldn't appear "too young." I have been 35 for twelve years now. When I actually turned 35, it seemed anticlimactic, since a version of me had already reached this plot point years ago.

I know this is true of them. We are who we say we are for 80 minute sessions, two days a week, 15 weeks of a semester. There's a level of trust here between storyteller and audience. The stories I tell them - the ones where I appear more interesting or lighten the mood have been amalgamations of my life experiences... so much so that I forgot the original thread.

When I started to write this, I was thinking of the students I lost over the years. Then the pandemic hit. And I watched my students pack up their things to head home, confused and lost. Their "home" became a Zoom background fixture and I watched them struggle to meld together the identities they've created and the ones their parents still expected them to have.

I tried to keep a class together. It's hard to build an imaginary fire through a series of screens. I am here as I have always been - but now I am in the castle's largest room filled with hay, not sure who I am waiting for or why this spinning wheel is here.

Before we left campus, I stood in front of my last class of the day. At this point, the plan was to stay past spring break for two weeks. I knew I wasn't going to see them again after this point.

Eight students out of sixteen stared back at me.

"Professor, do you know what's happening?"

(nervous glances are exchanged, bodies become anxious as they wait for an answer)

"No. I know what you know."

(partly true)
(expectant silence)

"But I do know that we know nothing. So we need to prepare for something. I think you all should prepare to stay home longer than two weeks."

(silence that is processing, thinking of its next words)

"It's that bad?"

(a new voice. The one who doesn't talk now suddenly needs to say something into this classroom space, one last time)

"It isn't great. But you will all be fine, I know this. I do recommend staying informed and bringing home whatever you can. This isn't going away, okay?"

"Professor, you were the first person being honest with us."

I feel ashamed at this moment. My "honesty" is nothing but vague talk, pointed in a randomized direction and hoping it sticks. What I want to say, what I need to say, isn't here right now. It's lost in a cultural noise of news notifications, the need to constantly be moving, the lack of answers. At the beginning of the semester, I told them we would find the answers together. At best, I told them what I didn't know because they deserved whatever I had left to give them.

The semester ended and we all parted ways. Some reached out with kind words and others wished me a good summer. All in all, it was a standard goodbye, minus the face-to-face interaction. My class is a blip in a larger pandemic narrative, I know this. All of the assignments and deadlines have been checked off the list. But we didn't set out what we planned to do. Luckily, I am the only one who knows.

I go back in the fall - maybe.

I will teach face-to-face once again - maybe.

Wherever I am, I will need to be vigilant about my health and the health of my students, physically, mentally, and emotionally. Some things don't change, but the stakes have been getting higher and higher lately.

I hope I have enough stories to tell.

In my classes on trauma theory, we discuss the new normal. I know it will get here when it's good and ready - it does not care for mortal sensibilities. As always, my students will move on and their names and faces will fade from memory until their stories are part of my classroom persona. Despite this, I will try my best to remember them all. Mnemosyne is laughing at me and my fool's errand.

In the privilege of their youth, I am quite sure they do not think of a writing class with a weird professor all those years ago. This is the plight of all educators - they leave and we stay, hoping the radio silence that follows is good news and not the worst story imaginable.

For now, I will throw another log on that imaginary fire and pretend the flames I conjured are just enough. At least, for a brief moment, I can keep us all warm.

Furious Lit Contributors

Shannon Frost Greenstein

Shannon Frost Greenstein resides in Philadelphia with her children, soulmate, and cats. She is a Pushcart Prize and Best of the Net nominee, a Contributing Editor for *Barren Magazine*, and a former Ph.D. candidate in Continental Philosophy. Shannon served as writer–in–residence for the Sundress Academy for the Arts and was selected as a NASA social media intern for an official launch from Cape Canaveral. Her work has appeared in *McSweeney's Internet Tendency*, *X–R–A–Y Lit Mag*, *Cabinet of Heed*, *Spelk Fiction*, *Scary Mommy*, and elsewhere.

Find Shannon online at:
twitter.com/mrsgreenstein
facebook.com/shannongreenstein
instagram.com/zarathustra_speaks
shannonfrostgreenstein.com

Adam Wilson

A former editor for Twofold Comics and 215 Ink, Adam Wilson is one of the co–founders of Read Furiously. As a comic writer, Adam has published two graphic novels: *Brian & Bobbi* and *In the Fallout*. He co–writes the graphic novel series *The MOTHER Principle,* and his short stories have been featured in numerous anthologies. Adam is also a contributor to the Read Furiously One 'n Done series which features his first novella *What About Tuesday* and his graphic novella *Helium.* Adam lives in West Trenton with his wife, and fellow Read Furiously founder, Samantha Atzeni, their son, and cat.

Find Adam online at:
instagram.com/amwilson81
asplashpage.blogspot.com

Victoria Tracy

Victoria is a freelance writer, poet, and avid coffee drinker from Raleigh, NC. This is the first anthology her work will be featured in. When she's not writing, Victoria spends her time enjoying art museums and reading horror novels.

Find Victoria online at:
instagram.com/torietracy

Margaret Montet

Margaret Montet's narratives of place blend memoir, research, nature, and the arts. She's a reference librarian at Bucks County Community College and a graduate of the Pan European MFA Program at Cedar Crest College. Margaret blends these skills when speaking about writing, speaking, travel, and music–related topics in the Central Jersey/Southeastern Pennsylvania region. Her creative nonfiction has been published in the anthologies *The World Takes: Life in the Garden State* and *Flying South*, as well as many journals: *Dragon Poet Review, The Bangalore Review, Pink Pangea* and others. *Nerd Traveler*, a collection of travel essays, will be published soon with Read Furiously.

Find Margaret online at:
twitter.com/margaretmontet
instagram.com/margiquilt
margaretmontet.com

Camden Michael Jones

As of June 2020, Camden Michael Jones has earned his BA in English Literature and History from Western Oregon University. He plans to continue his education with an MFA of Poetry or Creative Writing after a gap year or two. During the summers, Camden is a wildland firefighter and many of his poems concern his time on the job, but his multifaceted personality is evident in the diversity of subjects he writes about. He married his best friend in October 2019, and they live in Eastern Oregon with their cat, O'Malley.

Find Cameron online at:
instagram.com/camden.m.jones

Claire Tomasi

Claire Tomasi is a writer, cartoonist, and mental health advocate. Her comics focus on memoir, lifestyle, and growing up in New Jersey. She lives in New York City with her dog, Ticket.

Find Claire online at:
instagram.com/alittleclaireity
clairetomasiart.com/

Susan Padron

Susan Padron is an intuitive personal stylist. Susan helps women work through limiting beliefs, so that they can start showing up as their best self by expressing their personality with personal style. In addition to working with personal clients, Susan is a certified fashion stylist, who also enjoys doing wardrobe styling for commercial photo shoots.

Find Susan online at:
facebook.com/SusanPadronstylist
instagram.com/susanpadron_stylist

Carolyn Banks

Photography has been a huge part of Carolyn's life since she was a kid. She remembers playing with her Dad's Kodak Instamatic camera before she was old enough to go to school. This fascination grew throughout her childhood and then into the dark room in college. She ultimately gained a Mass Communications/Advertising degree from Towson University. After college, she worked for several ad agencies before making photography a full time career. She's never looked back.

Find Carolyn online at:
facebook.com/sophiagracephotophilly
instagram.com/sophiagracephoto
sophiagracephotos.com

Elliott Stegall, PhD.

Dr. Elliott Stegall is a retired professor of the humanities with courses taught at FSU and at Northwest Florida State College. His screenplay *Hell Hath No Fury* is available on Amazon. His stage play *Oh, Brother!* was produced at the University of West Florida. He appears in several short films on the Internet, including *Fall of a Saga, Sacred Cow,* and *Sins of the Mother.* He is presently working on a novel, *Immortal.*

Jo Freehand

Jo Freehand is a poet and multi–media artist who lives with her partner and a large community of woodland critters in Bucks County, Pennsylvania. She is a certified Embodied Present Process facilitator, as well as creator and facilitator of *It Feels So Write: A Whole Body Creative Writing Workshop.* She is Contributing Editor for River Heron Review. Jo is founder of Peace of Paper, a nonprofit organization that collects writing and drawing supplies and distributes them to children and adults for creative expression in times of distress, including unstable housing situations, poverty, and following violence and trauma.

Find Jo Online at:
jofreehand.com

Matt Lydon

Matt Lydon started out as an idea, who then became a child. After some time, he grew to adulthood. Sometime during that, he began writing stories. This is one of them.

Find Matt online at:
facebook.com/theemattlydon

twitter.com/theemattlydon
instagram.com/theemattlydon
mattlydonwrites.com

Candice Lola

Candice Lola is a fiction writer and essayist based in New York City. She is a graduate student in NYU's Experimental Humanities program, focusing on Creative Writing and Human Rights. She is also closet gothic fantasy fan, a sommelier of cheap wines, a burner of fine foods, and a fangirl of all things geeky. Her stories are heavily allegorical representations of happenings in her life.

Candice Lola has published work with *Indigo & Midnight*, *The Huffington Post*, *Medium*, *In The Words of Womyn (ITWOW) Journal*, and other literary publications.

Find Candice online at:
facebook.com/candi.lola
twitter.com/candice_lola
instagram.com/candice_lola
candicelola.com

Samantha Atzeni

Samantha Atzeni is a writer of prose, comics, and academic scholarship. She has a BA in Professional Writing and MA in English from The College of New Jersey. She is the co-founder and Editor-in-Chief of Read Furiously and currently teaches post-modernism, Holocaust studies, superheroes, and pop culture at The College of New Jersey. Samantha Atzeni lives in New Jersey with her husband, comic writer Adam Wilson, their son, and their cat Alaska who has yet to become internet famous, despite their best efforts.

Find Samantha online at:
instagram.com/smatzeni
satzeni.com

What is a MuZine?

In the earliest days of Read Furiously, we cut our teeth vending tables at the Trenton Punk Rock Flea Market, a celebration of independent DIY culture. Leading up to those events, the Read Furiously editorial and design teams would spend weeks before the shows collaborating on handmade zines that celebrate the values we as a company hold dear. Seen as musings on literature, storytelling, book culture, MuZines became a staple of the Trenton Punk Rock Flea Market experience for us. Mashing poetry with photography, we would hold Late Night Zine Parties - printing, cutting, pasting, and folding around a table filled with pizza and coffee into the early hours of the morning.

They were exclusive items, only available in person at the flea markets, or through us on our website, but now as Read Furiously continues to grow and we launch our new anthology series, *Furious Lit*, we wanted to take a moment to revisit those zines and offer readers an opportunity to see a few of our favorites. Many of them are no longer in print, some of the original files have even been lost as we've transferred offices and upgraded computer software. But the heart and soul that guided us in those late night MuZines-making parties still embody everything we do at Read Furiously. We celebrate books, we celebrate reading, and we celebrate you, our Furious Readers.

And with that, we hope you enjoyed this little glimpse into Read Furiously's past, as we look out into a bright future ahead of us.

With love and Books!

More from Read Furiously

A Note to Our Furious Readers

From all of us at Read Furiously, we hope you enjoyed *Tell Me A Story*, the first volume of our themed anthology series *Furious Lit*.

There are countless narratives in this world and we would like to share as many of them as possible with our Furious Readers.

It is with this in mind that we pledge to donate a portion of these book sales to causes that are special to Read Furiously and its creators. These causes are chosen with the intent to better the lives of others who are struggling to tell their own stories.

Reading is more than a passive activity – it is the opportunity to play an active role within our world. At Read Furiously, its editors and its creators wish to add an active voice to the world we all share because we believe any growth within the company is aimless if we can't also nurture positive change in our local, national, and global communities. The causes we support are not politically driven, but are culturally and socially-based to encourage a sense of civic responsibility associated with the act of reading. Each cause has been researched thoroughly, discussed openly, and voted upon carefully by our team of Read Furiously editors.

To find out more about who, what, why, and where Read Furiously lends its support, please visit our website at readfuriously.com/charity

Happy reading and giving, Furious Readers!

Read Often, Read Well,
Read Furiously!

www.ingramcontent.com/pod-product-compliance
Lightning Source LLC
Chambersburg PA
CBHW061919130726
47908CB00017B/2472